Rick Hansen

A Life in Motion

Don Quinlan

Fitzhenry & Whiteside

Published in Canada by Fitzhenry & Whiteside, 195 Allstate Parkway, Markham, Ontario L3R 4T8
Published in the United States by Fitzhenry & Whiteside, 311 Washington Street, Brighton, Massachusetts 02135

www.fitzhenry.ca   godwit@fitzhenry.ca

10 9 8 7 6 5 4 3 2 1

Library and Archives Canada Cataloguing in Publication
Quinlan, Don, 1947-
Rick Hansen: a life in motion / Don Quinlan.
ISBN 978-1-55455-195-8 (bound).--ISBN 978-1-55455-196-5 (pbk.)
1. Hansen, Rick, 1957–   —Juvenile literature. 2. Paraplegics—Canada—Biography—Juvenile literature.
3. Athletes with disabilities—Canada—Biography—Juvenile literature. 4. Wheelchair sports—Juvenile literature.
I. Title.
RD796.H35Q56 2011   j632.4'3092   C2011-905806-5

Publisher Cataloging-in-Publication Data (U.S.)
Quinlan, Don, 1947-
Rick Hansen : a life in motion / Don Quinlan.
[72] p. : ill. (some col.) ; cm.—A larger than life biography.
Includes bibliographical references and index.
Summary: Rick Hansen suffered a spinal cord injury at the age of 15 after a car accident. But that didn't stop him
from becoming a wheelchair basketball player in the Paralympics during the 1980s or from raising money and
awareness for spinal cord research through his "Man in Motion" tour. Hansen's activism and the foundation he
created after the tour continue to this day.
ISBN: 978-1-55455-195-8
ISBN: 978-1-55455-196-5 (pbk.)
1. Hansen, Rick, 1957-   —Juvenile literature. 2. Paraplegics—Canada—Biography—Juvenile literature.
3. Athletes with disabilities—Canada—Biography—Juvenile literature.
I. Title. II. A larger than life biography.
623.43092 dc23   RD796.H35Q56 2012

Fitzhenry & Whiteside acknowledges with thanks the Canada Council for the Arts, and the
Ontario Arts Council for their support of our publishing program. We acknowledge the financial support
of the Government of Canada through the Canada Book Fund (CBF) for our publishing activities.

Cover and interior design: Darrell McCalla
Cover image: Rick Hansen Foundation
Printed in China by Sheck Wah Tong Printing Press Ltd.

Contents

To the many heroes and difference makers across Canada.

Don Quinlan

Larger than Life

What makes a person "larger than life?" It certainly does not only refer to physical size, although personal strength may be part of the story. Maybe it has something to do with your own particular characteristics and skills. To some, it may involve facing great challenges and earning hard-fought victories. It could also refer to the fact that your fellow citizens, in your own country or around the world, look to you for guidance or inspiration.

Raising the Issue

This is the story of a great struggle to overcome physical, emotional, and psychological injuries; to turn disability into ability; and to ensure fairness for all. More than that, it is a story of personal triumph and athletic victory. It is a journey from a terrible truck accident deep in the interior of British Columbia to a successful world tour that raised millions of dollars and raised hope for millions of people. It is the true, larger-than-life story of a great Canadian—Rick Hansen.

Chapter One

A Boy's Life

Small Town Boy

Rick was an active youngster eager to explore the world around him.

Rick Hansen was born in Port Alberni, British Columbia on August 26, 1957. He was the oldest of four children. His family moved often and he spent time in several BC communities, including Port Alberni, Fort St. John, Abbotsford, and then Williams Lake. All were smaller towns located in or near the breathtaking landscapes of British Columbia. Rick's early years were spent growing up near surging rivers and deep lakes teeming with salmon and trout. It is no wonder he was fishing by the age of three—a passion that he pursues to this very day. Rick's world included a rich rainforest of giant trees and high meadows surrounded by beautiful, imposing mountains. It was a dream world for an active youngster eager to learn and master a full range of sporting and outdoor adventures.

Rick was the first born in a family of four children. Here, his parents, Joan and Marvin Hansen, are flanked by their children from left to right—Cindy, Brad, Christine, and Rick.

A Different Life

In many ways, Rick grew up in a more freewheeling frontier environment than most young Canadians. He had little knowledge of great urban centres, crowded downtowns, and spreading suburban malls.

His world was the vast, sprawling outdoors and the small towns where he grew up hunting, fishing, and playing any active sport that he came across.

Freedom and Independence

From a very early age, Rick was independent. He admits to being somewhat aloof from the rest of his family and being a trifle headstrong— even unruly—at times.

Originally built during the Gold Rush, Williams Lake is now a centre for tourism, forestry, mining, and ranching.

Rick explains, "I moved around a lot as a kid due to my dad's job and there never seemed to be time to make close friends growing up. I wasn't a great communicator and didn't let too many people get that close to me. I wanted to be in the outdoors fishing, riding my bike, and climbing trees. I was stubborn, competitive and wanted to make my own rules. I think it was challenging for my parents to try and raise a kid who craved so much independence."

Being first born probably encouraged Rick's sense of independence. Moving often while he was young also meant that he felt few roots or restraints. He did not really like school or going to church; he was much more inclined to fish or play sports. Likewise, he did not spend a lot of time at home and became more difficult as he grew into his teens. However, school did bring good friends and organized sports that offered discipline and a sense of community. Rick was also a natural leader with a zest for adventure.

Much of life is about choices—some simple, some not so simple. Some choices have few consequences while others are life changing. In the summer of 1973, when Rick was only fifteen years old, he made a fateful choice. He was invited to a special volleyball clinic near his home. The clinic was held to help kids prepare for the opportunity to play for the Pacific Rim and Canada Games teams. Rick

> **"If you could throw it, hit it, bounce it, chase it or run with it, I wanted to play it and usually, I could do it pretty well."[1]**
>
> *Rick Hansen*

loved the sport—he was good at it. Going to the clinic should have been the obvious choice. However, he decided to go on a week-long fishing adventure with his two buddies, Don Alder and Randy Brink, instead—from Williams Lake to Bella Coola, some 467 kilometres (290 miles) away, with no adult supervision.

Chapter Two
The Day that Changed Everything

The beautiful stretch of land between Kamloops and Prince George, British Columbia, is known as the Cariboo.

A Fateful Choice

ick and his friends planned a perfect boys' adventure: a week-long fishing trip, all on their own terms. They would drive a truck hundreds of kilometres through some of the most beautiful landscape the province of British Columbia had to offer. No real rules and no adult supervision—just freedom, fun, and fishing.

Their trip would take them to exotic locales like One Eye Lake, Riske Creek, and Bella Coola before heading home to Williams Lake. The roads were twisted and difficult. The plan was to drive when they wanted to drive and rest when they wanted to rest.

Today, frankly, some of what the boys planned would be deemed highly unwise, even illegal. The total lack of adult oversight would be a great concern. However, the headstrong Rick and his friends lived in another place and another time when these sorts of adventures were common.

They fished, hiked, laughed, and had a blast. Better yet, they were catching fish—lots of fish. Early in the trip, they came across a road accident. A Jeep had flipped over and tossed out several passengers. The boys quickly helped the injured passengers and took them for help. Later, they came across a fellow with a flat tire. The boys eagerly pitched in and helped change it.

The boys eventually decided to head back. It was in the middle of the night on a high canyon road with deep cliffs on either side. They were tired. The road was dark. At one point it appears they all fell asleep—including the driver—and the truck ran right off the mountain road. Luckily, the truck landed on one of the few ledges in the area and a passing dump truck pulled them to safety, and drove them to a store owned by Randy's father.

The dump truck driver offered to drive them back home to Williams Lake, but Rick and his good friend

Don Alder decided it would be more fun to hitchhike on their own. Randy decided to stay behind at his father's store. Nowadays, hitchhiking is both risky and illegal in most parts of Canada. But that day, the boys stuck out their thumbs and watched car after car go by. Just as they were about to give up on getting a ride, a truck passed. Then it squealed to a halt. The driver was the same fellow that they had helped earlier with the flat tire.

The Crash

What seemed like a lucky break soon proved disastrous. To begin with, the driver had been drinking. Second, rather than sitting securely in seats with seatbelts, Rick and Don were riding in the back of a pickup truck piled high with loose stuff that bounced and shifted with every bump and turn on the gravel road. Rick climbed up on a toolbox and fell asleep.

Looking back, Rick says, "I could give you a dozen reasons why it should never have happened, point to a dozen places where choices—simple choices—logically could have been made another way, and I'd be walking today instead of wheeling. I've had a lot of hospital time on a lot of sleepless nights to count them…All that matters is that on June 27, 1973, on a hot summer evening around 8 P.M., I was bouncing along on a gravel road in the back of a pickup truck with my buddy, Don Alder. Two kids—me fifteen, him sixteen—hitchhiking home from the kind of week city kids can only dream about. And everything fell apart."[1]

Rick awoke to skids, swerves, and screams. The truck flipped, and Rick and Don were sent hurtling out of the truck. Both thought that they were going to die. Rick landed on the toolbox and heard a sickening crunch before blacking out.

"I woke up and thought, 'Hey I'm alive!' Then I thought, 'Whoa! Something's wrong here. Something's definitely wrong.' Because I tried to move and I couldn't.

"There were boxes and junk all over me. I was propped up against this toolbox and I couldn't move. It didn't hurt—not then. I guess I was in shock. All I remember clearly is the dust settling around me. But suddenly there was this searing pain—pain like I'd never felt before. And I'd never in my life been so afraid."[2]

Chapter Three

The Struggle to Build a New Life

A young Rick looked ahead at a world of endless challenges.

Rick was taken first to Cariboo Memorial Hospital in Williams Lake, but he was so badly injured that he was transferred to Royal Columbian Hospital in New Westminster BC—a long seven-hour trip by ambulance.

Many of Rick's friends came came to visit and he would try to be upbeat when they were around. His parents visited as well, but in his own words, he "dumped all over them" as they tried to help him face his fears and frustrations.

Rick liked his nurses who were young, pretty, and kind to him. He even felt that they spoiled him. Sometimes, they would smuggle him into the nurses' quarters to hang out, chat, and play music—after all, some of them were only two years older than he was.

Rick absolutely refused to accept the doctors' diagnosis that he would never walk again. He was rude and abrupt to his doctors. Although he was often an unruly and rambunctious patient, Rick's bravado covered up his great physical and emotional pain. Late at night, he had to face his dark fears. Sometimes he threw up or cried. Much of the time, he was deeply unhappy.

"After my injury, I was very discouraged and frustrated," says Rick. "I constantly compared my life before I was injured with my new reality and found it lacking. Once I could see the possibilities and stopped comparing, it was easier for me to face the challenge of my new situation. I have had some amazing experiences since my injury, and I wouldn't trade them for anything."

Rick at Home

Once Rick was able to return home from the hospital, the new reality of his disability was a huge strain on the patience, energy, and resources of his entire family.

While Rick was devastated by his injuries, he was not the only one to suffer. It is hard to know how his parents must have felt. His younger brother and sisters had a painful adjustment too. "It was harder for my brother and sisters though," says Rick. "Being young, I think they always expected me to walk again—that some doctor would come and operate and I'd get the use of my legs back. I think for the first few years, they really thought of my wheelchair as something temporary. Being seventeen and in the mind frame I was at the time, I didn't express my feelings very well to any of them."

The Spinal Cord

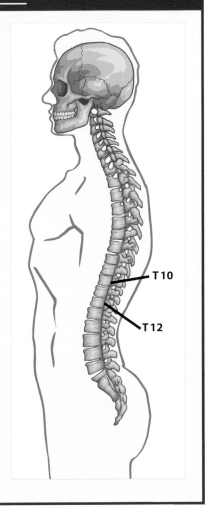

The spinal cord is about 18 inches long and extends from the base of the brain, down the middle of the back, to about the waist. Your spinal cord is the lifeline that connects your brain to all parts of your body. The bones of your spine have the important job of protecting this vital cord. Most spinal cord injuries are serious, if not catastrophic: When the spine and cord are damaged, then the signals from your brain cannot reach the rest of your body properly, so some body parts will not function well, or at all.

In general, the higher the break point or spinal cord injury, the more bodily dysfunction the injured person will suffer. The lower the injury, the fewer bodily functions are affected.

There are about 1,400 spinal cord injuries in Canada every year. Although scientists still cannot fully heal spinal cord injuries, research and rehabilitation are reducing the impact caused by these serious injuries.

Rick's spine was broken in two lower places (T10 and T12) and his spinal cord was badly damaged. However, he had full use of his upper body. This was to be an important factor in Rick's recovery.

Rick's family life had been less than perfect, although his family clearly loved and supported him. He was a bit of a loner and was not as close to his family as one might expect. "Unfortunately, my family took the brunt of the frustration and anger I had at my new reality," Rick explained. "Outwardly, I would be positive and brave, telling people this wasn't going to slow me down, but within the four walls of my house, I really let my true feelings fly. Every time I would face a challenge, I would think to myself, 'this is forever, it's going to be this way forever...' and the anger would bubble up again. It was a process I had to work through mentally and being seventeen years old didn't help. I was tough on them for sure."

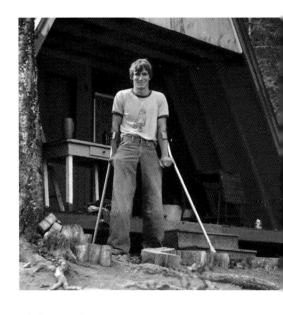

After strenuous rehabilitation, Rick returned home.

Moreover, Rick's mother and father did not always get along. But they were willing to sacrifice a great deal, and likely stayed together longer than they might have because of their son's accident. In fact, while Rick was at university a few years later, his parents separated and eventually divorced.

At first, Rick's house was totally inaccessible by wheelchair. It is no wonder that one of his passions has been to raise awareness for accessibility. Over time, Rick's family made many adjustments to the house to make it easier for him to live there. For a boy who was used to leaping stairs, the need for crutches and braces to get up and down stairs was maddening and humiliating. "In the beginning," Rick recalls, "my parents were worried over any thump they heard, knowing I had fallen trying to climb the stairs or

> **"When I needed them, they were always there. I loved them then, I love them now, and I always will."[1]**
>
> *Rick Hansen*

bashed my head into a wall trying to get into my braces. But once they got used to it and I got better skilled at getting around, life pretty much went on as before."

Rick fought the house and the house fought back. Both he and his house had the bruises and dents to show for their struggles. "To this day, there's a dent in the plaster shaped just like my forehead, next to the bed in one of the upstairs bedrooms."[2] Rick believes that in the struggle for dominance, the result was a tie. "The first thing I had to adjust to was a completely inaccessible house. There were stairs everywhere so I strapped on the braces and crutches and tackled them the way I did the stairs and hallways at rehab…I must have ripped out the banisters about once a week trying to haul myself up to the living room and down to the basement. It was winter too, and the ice and snow constantly conspired to land me headfirst into a snow bank. It was so maddening and frustrating I could barely stand it. Here was this intensely independent kid used to doing things for himself and now he had to rely on his family for everything. It was a mental struggle I had to overcome."

With Friends

One thing Rick had in abundance was good friends who did not abandon him. Rick soon learned how lucky and rich he was. His friends stood by him, involved him in virtually all activities, helped him with his problems, and showed him that not everything had changed. Rick admits that, at first, he was not the easiest person to be with. He was angry, moody, stubborn and self-conscious. At times he was overcome by powerful emotions: "There was an adjustment for everyone at first but once the initial shyness was out of the way, my friends were the same as always. I got my dad to hang a trapeze from the ceiling in the basement so I could hang on with one hand and stand on my braces, playing ping pong with my other hand. Don and Randy would come over and we'd play for hours.

"That first Christmas after the accident, a bunch of kids decided to go to Blue Lake for the weekend but there was so much snow, I couldn't make it. They got a toboggan, grabbed the ropes, and hauled me in. We could have had the greatest time but I was sulking because I had to be tobogganed in. My friends were fine—it was me who had to change my attitude."

Rick overcame the challenges of his injuries and learned how to have fun again. Here he is ice fishing at Christmas in 1977.

Over time, the love, respect, and patience Rick's friends showed him helped them all return to the fun of his pre-accident days. "[My friends] were there for me just as they were before the accident. They knew when to back off and when to tell me I was being a jerk. They were never condescending about it. They didn't ignore the accident, but they didn't let it define me either. If anyone was self-conscious about it, it was me. When I think back now, I couldn't have asked for a better group of friends to go through that transition with. Especially Don, who had his own guilt about the accident, having walked away without a scratch. I needed those friends immensely, even if I couldn't express it."

For the young, healthy, athletic, physically capable Rick, attracting a girlfriend was not a big issue. However, after the accident, Rick was not as confident. He worried that no one would want to be around him, and that he was no longer desirable. Sports, driving, and even dancing seemed beyond him. He worried that if a girl showed interest, perhaps it was out of pity or that eventually she would want to date a more physically abled boy. Much to his surprise and delight, he soon learned that his insecurities belonged only in his head and not in his life; one day, an attractive girl asked him out on a date. For the rest of his youth, Rick enjoyed the company of friends and girlfriends. That part of his life was not lost in the accident.

Rick at School

School provided other challenges too. The fire of competition had burned bright in the young Rick Hansen. Gyms and playing fields had been scenes of success and victory. Entering this realm in a wheelchair or on braces was difficult at first, but he soon impressed everyone with wheelchair tricks like 180s and 360s.

When Rick finally went to his high school gym, after avoiding it for as long as he could, he saw his coach and his pals playing the sport he had enjoyed so much— volleyball. Fortunately, few people treated him any differently than they had before his accident; in fact, his coach went out of his way to ask Rick for help in assessing the players. Rick was overcome by emotion.

It would not be long before Rick was to return to gyms, fields, and tracks where he experienced once again the adrenaline rush of competition and the elation of victory. Rick was about to realize that his wheelchair was not his enemy. In fact, it was the key to future success and happiness.

"Sustaining a spinal cord injury and becoming a paraplegic completely changed my world," Rick says. "I had always been really active, playing sports or going on adventures with friends—so it took time to adjust to life at home using a wheelchair. I was devastated because I thought using a wheelchair meant I wasn't the same person I was before my injury; I thought people would treat me differently and I didn't like feeling dependent on others. But thanks to the support of good friends, family, and my coach, I soon realized a person is not defined by their disability—that my biggest hurdle was my own attitude. Once I shifted my perspective and changed how I approached challenges, I discovered I was still able to do a lot of the things I did before my injury."

Rick's friends never stopped supporting him.

Chapter Four

Saved by Sports

Here, Rick stands with the volleyball team he helped coach.

Role Models and Mentors

R ole models and mentors are important sources of guidance, assistance, and inspiration. Rick Hansen was fortunate to have generous and dependable people in his life who have helped him over the years. To this day, he is grateful for their efforts on his behalf and loyal to their vision and values.

The Coach

From the moment Rick gingerly re-entered his old gym, Coach Bob Redford was pushing him to use his experience and leadership to coach his fellow athletes. He discovered that he was, in fact, a very good coach. While helping to coach and train a girls' volleyball team, the always active and energetic Rick found himself having to push his wheelchair all over the court, driving hard to keep up with the able-bodied athletes. He quickly learned to master the wheels, built up his speed and strength, and reduced the impact of his disability.

Rick was never a passive coach. He was active and involved. The old competitive fires returned quickly. More importantly, this new outlet for his talents and energies helped him to recover his once-boundless confidence and courage. Thanks to Coach Redford's patience, encouragement, and support, Rick was able to see that

Bob Redford has been a lifelong friend of Rick's, with him every step of the way.

maybe there was a bright future for him after all. "The truth is, Rick wasn't that great an athlete in high school," recalls Bob Redford. "He was a good athlete—good co-ordination, good skills, highly coachable—but not great in the sense that he was going to be a pro or a superstar. He was a kid who played a lot of sports, at a better-than-average level, played them all, and worked his tail off to get better." [1]

The Old Man

One day, as Rick was going to school, an old man in a red convertible called out to him. That man was Stan Stronge, a former athlete who, like Rick, was now in a wheelchair. Stan would become the person who moved Rick's athletic horizons far beyond the confines of the little gym in Williams Lake.

Stronge had organized a variety of wheelchair sports in and around Vancouver, and he soon drew Rick into a brand new world of competition and excellence. Rick began with a table tennis competition in Seattle. Next he moved to a position with the Vancouver Cable Cars, a wheelchair basketball team, another one of Stan's creations. Rick also qualified for the National Wheelchair Games in tennis and basketball in Montreal. There, he was impressed by the range of sports and the excellent level of competition. Rick knew that the wheelchair was no longer a barrier to this new world; it was a vehicle to even greater competition and excitement.

Stan Stronge

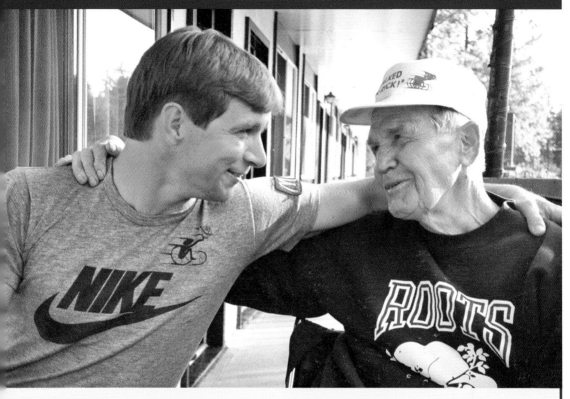

Rick could always depend on his loyal role model, Stan Stronge.

Stan Stronge was paralyzed when a tree fell onto his car during a storm in 1940. He had been a prominent soccer player and had recently married. There were few supports for paraplegics in those days. Stan responded to his life challenge by making no excuses. He moved on with his life. He turned to disability sports both as a player and an organizer. Stan was a pioneer in Canadian wheelchair basketball. He led the British Columbia team to six national championships from 1976 to 1982.

Stan also coached and managed numerous paraplegic swimmers to an international level of competition.

The Stan Stronge Therapeutic Pool in Vancouver was named in his honour by Premier Bennett in 1980. Stan died in 1993.

Later, Rick helped establish the Stan Stronge Wheelchair Basketball Fund. As Rick noted, "[Stan] searched for and reclaimed his life, he became happy and fulfilled, and he even made time to help others along the way."[2]

Chapter Five

Rick's Impossible Dream

Bitten once again by the bug of competitive sports, Rick Hansen never turned back to his post-accident gloom. He was a driven young man with a purpose and a plan.

School

Although the major focus of Rick's school years had been the love of sport and physical activity, both he and his family understood the value of a good education.

In 1976, when Rick enrolled in the Physical Education Faculty at the University of British Columbia (UBC), some people shook their heads. How could someone in a wheelchair expect to earn a degree in physical education? Rick recalls, "The greatest challenge was getting accepted into the program. I had to convince the admissions board that I could succeed when it had never been done before. They wouldn't let me in the first year, but thanks to my staff advisor, I got into the program in my second year."

Rick took on his physical challenges with gusto. UBC is built on steep hills, so even getting to class was a tough physical challenge. Rick changed attitudes at UBC, so people with disabilities were viewed on more equal terms. He also inspired structural changes that reduced the external barriers of doors, walkways, and washrooms so that the facilities were more accessible for those using wheelchairs.

Rick trained for sports with able-bodied, disabled, and temporarily injured athletes. While he continued training and coaching, he also focused on his studies. Then one day, he met a young athlete named Terry Fox who had lost his leg to cancer. Rick invited Terry to train with the university wheelchair basketball team: One of Canada's greatest athletic combinations was born. These two young men would later ignite the world with their incredible accomplishments.

A Remarkable Record

Rick's entry into the world of Paralympic and disability sports soon made him a front-page athletic personality in Canada, growing stronger, faster, and more determined. This was a Golden Age for the young athlete. However, the best was yet to come.

Terry Fox

Terry Fox is a true Canadian hero who has inspired generations of Canadians and others across the globe. While Terry ran on one real leg and one prosthetic leg, his Marathon of Hope took him from the shores of Newfoundland, to just outside of Thunder Bay—a remarkable distance of 5,374 kilometres (3340 miles)! Every year since his death, people across the world run and walk to continue raising funds for cancer research for the Marathon of Hope.

Rick mastered wheelchair basketball and volleyball quickly. He gained strength and speed. Next, he turned his attention to track and field, first with relays and then in the ultimate challenge—the marathon.

Rick was amazed at the speed and skill of a Newfoundlander named Mel Fitzgerald. Mel's body was an efficient racing machine. But he also redesigned wheelchairs. The first wheelchair races had been run with ordinary wheelchairs you might find in any hospital or rehabilitation facility. These wheelchairs were big and slow with an emphasis on safety, stability, and protection. But Mel had created "souped-up" chairs that were light and extremely fast. These speedsters were perfectly designed for sprinters and marathon

Souped-up wheelchairs redefined competitive racing.

athletes alike. "I truly believe Mel is the father of modern-day wheelchair racing," says Rick. "He was the first man to bring together the small push rims, the bigger wheels, the lightweight alloy chair frame, and the technique required to use them. After meeting Mel, I started to think about my wheelchair differently and got straight to work on building a new chair, using some of Mel's ideas and some of my own. As a result, I started winning marathons all over the world."

In 1979, Rick helped organize the world's first wheelchair marathon race. He entered the race and placed third. It was the beginning of a new life path. In 1982 at

Early Athletic Achievements

1976–1982: Six National Wheelchair Basketball Championships with the Vancouver Cable Cars

1979–1984: Winner, 19 international wheelchair marathons

1980: Outstanding Athlete of the Year, Canadian Wheelchair Sports Association; Paralympian (Gold 800 m, Silver 1,500 m and Bronze 4x100 m)

1982: Nine gold medals, nine records, Pan American Wheelchair Games; Silver medalist, Canadian Basketball Team, Pan American Games

1984: Paralympian (Gold 1,500 m, Gold Marathon and Silver 5,000 m); Participant, XXIII Olympic Games, Wheelchair Exhibition the Pan Am games in Halifax, Rick won an incredible nine gold medals. He blazed a trail of marathon victories across the globe, winning hard-fought competitions in England, Australia, North America, and Japan. From 1979 to 1983, Rick was unbeatable. One of his early crowning achievements was earning the Lou Marsh Award in 1983, two years before his Man In Motion World Tour. Named after a former *Toronto Star* sports editor, the Lou Marsh Trophy is awarded annually by a committee of sports journalists to Canada's outstanding athlete of the year. The award is special because it is so open—it can be won by man or woman, amateur athlete or professional star, rookie or veteran. The first winner in 1936 was Dr. Philip Edwards who won five Olympic medals in track and field.

Rick shared the honour of winning the Lou Marsh Award with "The Great One," Wayne Gretzky. At first, Rick's award was noted as an auxiliary, given out to an individual that didn't "quite fit the category." However, no one ever regarded it as such and even Wayne Gretzky indicated that he and Rick should be seen as equals. As Rick explains, "Winning the Lou Marsh Award was bittersweet. Of course, I was flattered and proud that it was awarded to Canada's Outstanding Male Athlete, but instead of sharing the award with Wayne, I received the 'auxiliary' award since I had a disability. I just wanted to be judged against other athletes as equals without need for a separate award. When Wayne accepted his award, he made a statement supporting and reaffirming my position, and I will always appreciate that. The hordes of media at the event made no mention of my award as being auxiliary, so that was one more step on the uphill climb to equality."

Rick drops the puck at a National Hockey League game. His co-winner of the Lou Marsh Award, Wayne Gretzky, was there to take the faceoff.

Problems with Success

However, even for Rick, such success can bring some problems. For a brief time, he neglected his training. Perhaps he felt that he was always going to win. He became a little careless and, in his own words, lazy. He began to lose. In 1983, he did not win the Orange Bowl World Championship Marathon Race—a race he had won three years in a row. He did not win in the Boston Marathon. Losing was a tough lesson: It was especially tough when Rick realized that he had lost because he had failed to respect his sport and his opponents. From that point on, Rick refused to let lack of preparation or a weak effort mar his career ever again.

While preparing for the 1984 Boston Marathon, Rick injured himself during training and could not participate. He was bitterly disappointed, but during his subsequent rehabilitation, he met Amanda Reid, a talented and beautiful physiotherapist who went on to play a huge role in his life.

"Meeting Amanda was, and still is, the most defining moment in my life," says Rick. "On the Tour, she was my physiotherapist, girlfriend, and rock of support. She always believed I could accomplish anything I set my mind to and never let me forget it."

Olympics

Although Rick relished competition and enjoyed victory, he strived for more than just personal achievement. He became an intelligent and persuasive spokesperson for the rights and needs of people with disabilities—not only in Canada, but across the world.

In 1984, Rick participated in the first Olympic Games Exhibition race for athletes with disabilities. Held in Los Angeles, this exhibition marked an important first step toward full acceptance and recognition of Paralympic sports by the International Olympic Committee, sports federations, and governments across the world. Rick would have a continuing connection to the Olympics and Paralympics.

The Impossible Dream

Victory after victory, tours to the far corners of the earth, and an increasingly busy lifestyle: You would think that Rick might have slowed down to pause and savour the fun and rewards of an active, successful life. But Rick was not done yet—not by a long shot. In fact, behind the scenes, he was already developing an ambitious project that would dwarf all his other achievements. It would challenge him to the core of his being and test his reserves of energy and health. Rick wanted to wheel all the way around the world—something no one had ever done, or likely even considered doing.

Rick's Man In Motion World Tour challenged him to his very core.

Where did Rick get this crazy idea? It began as a personal challenge back in the early days of rehab. He wanted to show the world he could "beat" his condition. At first, it wasn't about awareness or fundraising, but over time, and with some inspiration from his friend Terry Fox, the idea blossomed into something much bigger— something that might actually change the world. Through a worldwide series of marathons, Rick intended to raise public awareness of the issues facing people with disabilities, to educate people and governments about the need to remove barriers, and to ensure real equality between disabled and able-bodied people in every aspect of their lives. But Rick also dreamed of raising money to fund research for spinal cord injuries.

It seemed that Rick was chasing an impossible dream. At times, Rick may have even doubted himself—but not enough to stop.

Chapter Six
Conquering the World

RICK HANSEN
Man in motion
W·O·R·L·D·TOUR

My tour will cover 25,000 miles in 34 countries. The objectives of the tour are to demonstrate the abilities and skills of wheelchair bound people and to raise funds for spinal cord research and rehabilitation. Your pledges are greatly appreciated by myself and those who will be helped by the legacy this tour will leave behind. I am sure we can depend on you to send your pledged dollars to our Man in Motion office. It is located on the 21st floor at 1055 West Hastings, Vancouver, B.C. V6E 2E6. Phone (604) 687-5200.

Rick Hansen

McDonald's CARES

rom the time this incredible dream of wheeling around the world took root in Rick's mind, to the day that he and his team set off from the Oakridge shopping mall in 1985, Rick was thrust into a web of challenge and change. This new goal meant physical risks for his oft-injured body: perhaps greater disability or even death. It meant risking his professional position as *the* elite wheelchair marathoner in the world. He was also in the middle of earning a university degree in Physical Education. It was a huge risk for his personal and financial well-being both at that time and for the future. If he failed, his high-profile reputation might never recover. No wonder some people thought he was crazy.

Rick slowly worked out the details of the challenge and the reasons for this incredible journey. The memory of Terry Fox was never far from his mind. He had seen what a heroic effort by one person could do to galvanize Canadians into action. Rick's tour would have several demanding goals. He would raise awareness about the challenges and difficulties faced by people with disabilities all across the globe. He would raise funds for research and rehabilitation, and encourage recreation programs. Rick hoped to smash the very real physical and mental barriers that faced people with disabilities. He wanted his personal example to shift the focus of attention on the *possibilities* of the disabled, not the *problems*.

Facing the Challenges

In surviving his accident, Rick had already succeeded against enormous odds. He had returned to school and become an elite athlete. But, the Man In Motion dream would soon tax his body, mind, and spirit to their limits. In fact, Rick hoped to push his chair for 40,072 kilometres (24,900 miles) around the globe—a distance equal to the circumference of the earth! He planned to visit 34 countries in less than 2 years. The original scheme required him to wheel through 3 marathons a day—

about 126 kilometres (78 miles). This worked out to nearly 50,000 strokes of his wheels each and every day. No wonder many worried that he would not be able to complete the tour.

The physical challenge was frightening, but there were many other issues, too. Rick had to find a team to accompany him, to plan events, to help collect money, to find routes and hotels, and to prepare food. His body needed to be maintained and fine-tuned as much as his wheels did. He needed money to run the tour and he planned to raise more for spinal cord research along the way. How would it be collected and accounted for? Could he find enough good people to travel with him in a van in such close and cramped conditions? Who would run the tour from home in Canada? Who would organize publicity? This was a world without the Internet, smart phones, or social networking. So telling Rick's story would be a huge challenge, especially when he'd be travelling to so many foreign countries. There were many difficult questions and few easy answers.

As the questions and issues mounted, many of Rick's friends and advisors told him to wait until everything was properly organized. But with each new day more issues seemed to arise; the chance of actually *starting* the tour seemed to be under threat. At one point, Rick simply decided on the launch date for the tour: March 21, 1985. So, on that day, an inexperienced, somewhat unprepared, and shakily organized little band of believers departed from the Oakridge mall in Vancouver.

Looking back, Rick explains, "I had such mixed emotions that day at Oakridge mall—excitement that we were finally leaving after all the planning, trepidation because I was embarking on such a life-changing journey, and sadness at having to say good-bye to all of my family and friends who had come out to see me off. It was especially hard to say goodbye to Amanda as our relationship was so new; I just wanted to be with her and couldn't imagine not seeing her for 18 months. Would our feelings stand up to the separation? Would she be waiting for me when I came back? Was it even fair to ask her to?"

The first day was full of mishaps and little accidents but Rick and his team never looked back. It was "game on" for the greatest adventure and the toughest challenge of their lives. The Man In Motion World Tour (MIMWT) had officially begun.

The Team

Rick always knew that he would never succeed alone. He needed to build a team to support him. Slowly and after several mistakes, he did find the right team to share his challenges and dreams. In particular, there was Don Alder, Rick's life-long friend. During the tour, he was busy keeping Rick's much-worn and damaged equipment in shape. Tim Frick had known Rick for years and served as friend, coach, and tour coordinator for much of the difficult, complicated journey.

> **"I had an amazing team. They challenged, encouraged and supported me and asked nothing in return. I feel incredibly privileged to have had them with me."**
>
> Rick Hansen

And eventually, Amanda Reid joined them, serving as physiotherapist and terrain analyst. She also became the love of Rick's life and later, his wife.

Rick's team was the backbone of the Man In Motion World Tour.

At the outset of the tour, Rick missed Amanda terribly. But then, very early on, he damaged his wrists and fingers, so he asked her to come down to help him. He also recognized that he needed her for emotional support. Amanda was the only one he could fully open up to, to talk out his fears and frustrations. It wasn't always easy for them, of course, and their relationship was tested over the long months on the road. They were usually tired, living in cramped conditions and sometimes sick; they rarely had time alone. In the end, however, the challenges made their bond stronger.

Tour Highlights

Rick and his crew wheeled out of the Oakridge shopping centre full of hope and energy. They were tested very quickly. The following are just a few of the memorable highlights of this amazing journey across the world.

The United States

The first part of the tour stretched down the west coast from Vancouver, British Columbia, to San Diego, California, then swung east to Miami, Florida. One of the first challenges was the gruelling ascent up the Siskiyou Summit in Oregon. The tour organizers hadn't taken into consideration the severity of the headwinds that Rick would be facing—sometimes gusting at 40-65 kilometres an hour (30-40 miles an hour). This early challenge came after Rick had already pushed his tired body over a series of tough, high summits with demanding grades. Through the most difficult parts of the trip, Rick simply hunkered down and repeated "push, push," thousands of times.

A more pleasant part of the US tour was meeting David Foster and hearing the tour's official song, the famous theme from *St. Elmo's Fire*. In California, David met Rick and his crew and played a demo tape for them at a media event. That song on the tape grew to become a monster hit and was played live to an audience of 50,000 at the end of the tour in Vancouver.

Rick remembers the moment well: "Meeting David Foster was surreal. The fact that he wrote this gorgeous piece of music for the tour without ever having met me, and was able to give John Parr the inspiration he needed for the lyrics, still blows my mind. He couldn't have been more genuine and down to earth. He even got Lionel Richie to chat with me. It was unbelievable. When I hear the song now, it brings me right back to when I heard it the very first time, wheeling down the California coast, on the adventure of a lifetime."

David Foster wrote the tour's official song.

Europe

The European part of the tour began in disappointment but ended in triumph. The crowds were sporadic, the organization left much to be desired, and their motor home caught on fire. In Ireland, the team only collected $20 from the entire island! Rick and Amanda were seriously ill through the British Isles. They were still sick in France when it was discovered that their van had a leak in the exhaust system: As it turned out, everyone had been suffering from the effects of carbon monoxide poisoning.

> **"Nobody slept, the weather was abysmal, Don lost his passport, tensions were high, and everyone was grouchy. We were not a happy team, that's for sure. Not even close."**
>
> *Rick Hansen*

They continued their whirlwind tour of Europe, facing many stresses and strains, both on Rick's body and on the team's unity and morale. The countries whizzed by with varying degrees

In Vatican City, Rick had the honour of meeting Pope John Paul II.

of success. After a tough struggle across the Alps and then a triumphant tour of Yugoslavia, they finally reached Greece. From there, they went on to travel through the Middle East.

The Middle East

Rick and the crew had to carefully navigate the politics of this often tense and divided region. Security was tight because of ongoing Arab-Israeli tensions. However, they were usually greeted warmly, especially in Bahrain and Jordan, and they enjoyed success. A major event was crossing the Allenby Bridge from Jordan to Israel, which Rick also repeated as part of the 25th anniversary celebrations.

"Things went pretty well in the Middle East with lots of interviews, good television coverage, and plenty of people in wheelchairs joining me on the route," said Rick.

"A highlight for me was visiting the new Terry Fox Monument in Jerusalem that had just been built. Terry was with me in spirit always so it was a special moment."

Rick is greeted by some kangaroos in Australia.

Down Under—Australia and New Zealand

The "down under" part of the tour got off to a terrible start. The team was robbed on its first night in New Zealand; the stress of the tour and the long days of travelling in close quarters were taking their toll; and the team members were getting on each other's nerves. They were far from home, tired, and behind schedule. Rick and Amanda spent part of one night in a salad-tossing argument that fortunately ended with a hug.

They reached the 19,312 kilometre (12,000 mile) mark in Adelaide, Australia. The halfway point of the whole tour was celebrated just outside of Melbourne, Australia, with a formal crossing of a whipped-cream marking-line.

As the team members took stock of their efforts at the halfway point, they noted the following stats: 1,086 postcards written, 365 loads of laundry done, 63 flat tires changed, 63 pairs of gloves worn out, 100 rolls of tape used, one wheelchair worn out, 59 official receptions attended, and 7,180,800 wheelchair strokes completed.

"New Zealand was a turning point for the tour in that we consistently had a good crowd cheering us on and lots of company," said Rick, "especially kids, wheeling with us. I think the team was better at handling the logistics, too, getting on top of advance planning and organizing. I was overwhelmed with the response and support the Aussies were showing us. Mentally, I knew if I could just get halfway, I could finish what I started, having always split every wheeling challenge down the middle. I'd stuck to that thought process throughout the tour and now we had hit the biggest halfway of them all. I was elated."

Asia

China, South Korea, and Japan were some of the most successful sections of the tour. Although the team did not have much time, they managed to create quite an

"When I come back and it's all over…I want to be able to wake up in the morning…and see a picture of me in the wheelchair, sitting on the Great Wall of China…I want to be able to lie there for a minute, and stare at it, and remember what it took to get there, and remind myself that there are no walls too big to climb."[1]

impression. The Chinese in particular were generous hosts. One of the biggest problems for the team was surviving the enormous banquets that they faced every day.

When the tour finished up in Japan, Rick and the crew looked forward to the final leg of this remarkable journey awaiting them in North America. Home was still thousands of kilometres away, but the team knew the worst was over—except for one last Canadian winter!

Deng Pufang

One of the reasons for the MIMWT's success in the world's most populous nation was the effort of Deng Pufang, a son of the Chinese premier Deng Xiaoping. Deng Pufang suffered a broken back and was left paralyzed from the waist down during the Cultural Revolution in China. Like Rick and so many other paraplegics, he refused to give into his broken body by staying active and positive. With the help of his powerful father, Deng made sure that the Man In Motion World Tour was treated royally in China.

In 1984, Deng founded the China Welfare Fund for the Disabled and spent his life fighting for humanism in China.

In 2003, Deng was granted the United Nations Human Rights Prize for his work in protecting the rights of disabled people in China. He is the first Chinese citizen, as well as the first person with a disability in the world, to have received the United Nations Human Rights Prize.

Supporters follow Rick on his path in China.

Chapter Seven

A Canadian Hero

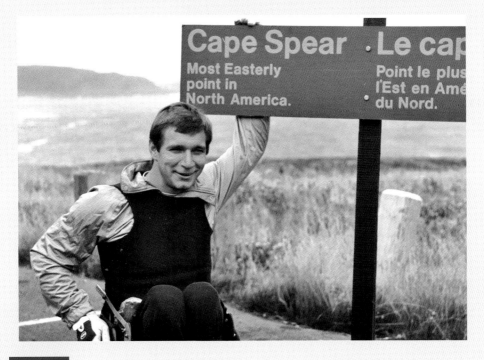

efore returning to Canada, the tour had a fast-paced ride up the east coast of the United States beginning in Miami, Florida. Although quick, this leg of the tour was a star-studded experience, attracting lots of media attention and interviews for Rick on American television.

Cape Spear, Newfoundland, August 25, 1986.

After 17 long, difficult, and often exhausting months of travel through 34 countries, the Man In Motion World Tour was finally back on home turf. Thousands of kilometres through some unforgiving terrain remained, but it was home, and Canada was waiting.

Rick Hansen was returning as a Canadian hero. While he had taken his message of hope to the world, every kilometre spent abroad had gathered even more recognition back home.

"Landing back in Canada after 17 months on the road was an extraordinary feeling. It felt so good to be home but I was also a little worried about the reception we would receive," says Rick. "Back then, media was nothing like what it is today and I truly had no idea if the tour would be embraced or even if there was any awareness about us at all. We were absolutely exhausted, but coming home really lit a fire under us. And the reception? It was magnificent, beyond anything I could have imagined. It felt like the whole country was behind us and what we were trying to achieve. I have never felt so proud to be a Canadian."

Rick's Man In Motion World Tour had already achieved one of its most important goals: to challenge assumptions about people with disabilities and to raise awareness of issues surrounding disabilities. But the team's second goal, to raise money for spinal cord research, was still woefully short. The hard, simple truth was that the tour was nowhere near reaching its goal of raising $10 million. In fact, in spite of all their efforts, as they returned home, the team members knew that they had only raised about $174,000. Being on the front pages of newspapers and being on posters was good, to a point, but $10 million was also extremely important so researchers could work toward permanent change and improvement in the field of spinal cord injuries. Happily, the legendary generosity of Newfoundlanders gave early proof that the tour would likely be a success. Within a few days of wheeling through a province where nearly a quarter of its citizens were out of a job, the tour organizers were stunned to raise over $97,000. It came in pennies, nickels, and dimes—whatever people had. Buckets were passed around. The cash came in so quickly that it was often temporarily stored in garbage bags!

On the personal side, Rick and Amanda found the time to get properly engaged in Shediac, New Brunswick. They had hoped to keep their engagement secret but word slipped out before they could tell their parents. Canada fell in love with the Rick and Amanda love story.

"My relationship with Amanda blossomed before the MIMWT," says Rick. "But really grew into something intense and life changing during the tour. How could it not after spending 24 hours a day with someone for two years straight? We both believed that if we could make it through that experience, we could make it through anything. Amanda (and the rest of the team) made it possible for me to complete the tour. Without her support, encouragement and professional care as a physiotherapist, I don't think I could have finished. I asked her to marry me in New Brunswick because I knew that as soon as the tour was over, I wanted to start our life together and not waste any time. I knew she was the love of my life."

Rick with Canadian Prime Minister Brian Mulroney in Ottawa on October 24, 1986.

As the team rolled through the Maritimes, the crowds grew larger and more enthusiastic. One memorable gathering in Truro, Nova Scotia, drew 10,000 fans and supporters. The days of trying to drum up interest were long gone. The major issues now became controlling the crowds and keeping to a strict schedule. Many towns, villages, and organizations wanted to meet Rick and the team, and hold fundraising events.

In Quebec, the team's lack of French made communicating with the citizens and media difficult. The team was never really able to reach the Québécois in quite the same manner that they did with English Canada. But Rick was still welcomed warmly into the province by wheelchair marathoner André Viger, a fellow member of the Terry Fox Hall of Fame.

When Rick rolled toward Ottawa, then-Prime Minister Brian Mulroney presented Rick with a cheque for $1 million from the Canadian government. He also spent time

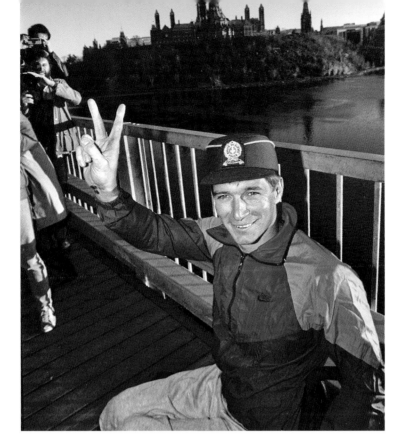

Rick on the bridge connecting Ottawa, Ontario, and Hull, Quebec, on October 24, 1986.

with Rick discussing accessibility issues for Canadians with disabilities. Being able to influence powerful politicians and leaders was a key part of Rick's efforts.

"For the Man In Motion Tour, awareness meant being a catalyst for good things to happen in a community, to help remove physical barriers and those erected by social attitudes. We were trying to be a messenger, to let people know that no matter what the form of disability—loss of limb, blindness, cerebral palsy, paralysis—everyone has hopes and dreams. And that my dream of wheeling around the world was no more significant than the dream of someone trying to make the long journey from a hospital bed to an electric wheelchair and thus lead a more independent life."

Ontario

By the time Rick and the team entered Ontario, they were well known and eagerly anticipated. At a giant rally in Toronto's Nathan Phillips Square, Rick spoke to an adoring throng of 100,000.

Hard climate often makes for beautiful scenery.

As Rick wheeled through a difficult Northern Ontario winter, he began to think about the spot near Thunder Bay where his friend and teammate, Terry Fox, was forced to end his Marathon of Hope. A hoped-for private visit to the Terry Fox monument outside of Thunder Bay was not to be as Rick was soon surrounded by eager media, but he sent his thoughts aloft and wheeled on. When the team left Ontario, it was more than halfway to its goal of $10 million. The wide-open West lay ahead with the Rocky Mountains looming as the last barrier before reaching home in British Columbia.

The West

Rick had feared a long, difficult winter, but fate was on the side of the Man In Motion World Tour: It seemed that even the weather in Canada was welcoming. That winter was milder than usual and seemed to cooperate when the team was on the road. In some places, Rick actually got tailwinds that made the wheeling easier.

The enthusiasm mounted and crowds continued to gather. When the team reached Alberta, Premier Don Getty pledged his government to match, dollar for dollar, the funds that Rick raised in that province. It was a welcome pledge that cost the Alberta government an eventual $2.5 million. A popular rock band, Loverboy, met Rick and made a pledge of $25,000 right then and there. The tour was clearly on a roll as it left Alberta and headed for home.

The Last Border

As Rick entered British Columbia, he was met by his mom and dad, family members, friends and supporters. It was an emotional moment. Premier Bill Vander Zalm also promised to match all money raised in BC. This generous gift eventually added up to $5.5 million. At that point, Rick knew that they were going to raise their goal of $10 million. In the end, the tour more than doubled the stated goal, raising over $26 million.

Home at Last

Although wheeling up and down mountain passes is no easy feat, the tour gained more and more momentum, and the smiles grew broader. The crowds, the donations, and Rick's fame grew as well. Although he had fought against too much personal recognition and credit, Rick was seen by millions around the world, in Canada, and in his native province, as a hero. For Rick, his new status was yet another challenge, and in many ways, a burden. He realized that there could never be a quiet return to a normal, everyday life; a whole new world of opportunity and responsibility was opening up.

BC Place

After the tumultuous welcome at Oakridge Centre in Vancouver, Rick was invited to a huge official closing ceremony at BC Place, complete with parades, presentations, music, and speeches.

Rick knew his dream had been worth it; he knew the team had made a difference. In all the noise and adulation, the kind words, hugs and well-wishing, he also knew that, in some ways, his life's work had just begun. As the banner declared, the end was just the beginning.

Fifty thousand fans roared their love and admiration for their hero at the official closing ceremony.

Chapter Eight

The End Was Just the Beginning

L ife was never to be the same for Rick Hansen after the successful conclusion of the MIMWT. Within six months, he and Amanda were married, and Rick began to think about how he would live the rest of his life.

Saying 'No' to Commercialism

Rick had become a Canadian hero. He was a powerful role model for people across the globe. That kind of fame and respect could easily have made him into a multimillionaire if he had chosen the path of easy money and celebrity. As tempting as it was, Rick felt it would be wrong to use his success, which after all did involve thousands of hard-working supporters, for his own advantage. He chose a different course for his future.

A New Path

Rick was named commissioner general of the Canadian pavilion at Expo 88 in Brisbane, Australia, where he represented Canada on the world stage.

When he returned from Expo 88 in 1989, Rick joined the University of British Columbia's Disability Resource Centre. His job was to direct initiatives to remove barriers for people with disabilities on both an international and national level. With one tiny office and no staff, Rick succeeded in developing a range of programs that made the university experience far more accessible. This organization is still a major force on the UBC campus today.

Achievements

Rick has continued to win awards. He was appointed to many committees and boards and was presented with honorary degrees from universities across Canada. He was made a member of the Terry Fox Hall of Fame, the BC Sports Hall of Fame, and the Canadian Sports Hall of Fame. In 1987, Rick was appointed a Companion of the Order of Canada, one of the highest honours in the country.

However, increasing public awareness of spinal cord injury, improving the lives of those suffering from this type of injury, contributing to research, and increasing accessibility were still top priorities following the MIMWT.

Rick Hansen Foundation

One of Rick's earliest steps was to organize the Rick Hansen Foundation in order to continue the work of the MIMWT. This organization has grown by leaps and bounds under Rick's leadership, and has raised an incredible $200 million for spinal cord injury-related programs. As the president, Rick has overseen some impressive achievements:

ICORD

Among the many organizations that are now located in this world-class centre is ICORD (International Collaboration on Repair Discoveries). ICORD is an organization with 300 researchers committed to finding solutions and strategies to help people with spinal cord injuries.

ICORD's groundbreaking research is shared with medical staff and researchers around the world.

Blusson Spinal Cord Centre

The Blusson Spinal Cord Centre is a result of cooperation between Rick and his team, the University of British Columbia, several health organizations and generous donors. The centre is the world's largest, most advanced, and most comprehensive facility devoted to spinal cord injury research and patient care. The $45 million, 6-storey building is a model of a fully accessible building. With special ramps, elevators with kick plates, and light switches set only three feet from the floor, it is a building designed for today, but serving as a model for an accessible future.

The Blusson Spinal Cord Centre remains a great testament to Rick's vision and ability to bring people and organizations together to do great things.

"I think today more people see the person first and not the disability," says Rick. "All I ever wanted was to be treated like everyone else, to be given the same opportunities to fully participate in my community, at school and in sports. I think we've come a long way in that recognition."

Wheelchair-accessible subways are just one of the many achievements in awareness about the position of people with disabilities.

Rick Hansen Institute

The SCI (Spinal Cord Injuries) Network was renamed the Rick Hansen Institute in January 2010. The institute is made up of a group of people with spinal cord injuries, researchers in the field, and people who provide help and assistance. The goal is to collaborate and share skills and knowledge to make life better for those suffering from spinal cord injury.

"Imagine a world where ...everyone living with a spinal cord injury enjoys a healthy, active and productive life and every newly injured person walks away."[1]

Rick Hansen

2010 Winter Olympics—Vancouver, BC

When Canada hosted the Winter Olympic and Paralympic Games in 2010, beautiful British Columbia was chosen as the venue. Rick Hansen, one of BC's favourite sons, was chosen to play a leading role. He was named mayor of the Olympic Village and torchbearer at the opening ceremonies. He also helped open the 2010 Winter Paralympics with a film tribute before he addressed the crowd. It seemed a suitable role. After all, Rick had taken Canada to the world during the MIMWT. Now, he could welcome the world to Canada. Although Rick's tour was nearly 25 years in the past, it was not yet over. Rick had a plan to relive the glory days and share it with a new generation.

Rick was chosen to be a torchbearer at the Winter Olympics in British Columbia.

Chapter Nine

Going the Distance, Looking to the Future

R ick Hansen is as active today as he was in his wheelchair-racing heyday. He has continued to build organizational structures and public awareness. Rick's stature in Canada and the world has continued to grow. At one point in 2010, serious consideration was given to having Rick serve as Canada's governor general. When Canadians were asked about some possible choices for the title, Rick's name topped the list. However, Rick felt he had much work that still needed to be done to raise

"Often people ask me if I would exchange the life I have led since my accident for the use of my legs. Sometimes they seem shocked or disbelieving when I invariably answer, 'No.'"[1]

funds for spinal cord research and to improve the lives of Canadians with disabilities.

A Personal Achievement

As important as the MIMWT and the work of the Rick Hansen Foundation are, Rick also enjoys a loving and supportive family life. With Amanda, he has raised three beautiful girls who are clearly his pride and joy. He is able to withdraw from the world and be a simple family man. He has always stated that his family has been central to his happiness.

> The **governor general** is Canada's most honoured representative. Originally, the governor general represented the British Crown in Canada. Today much of the governor general's role is ceremonial.

Rick and Amanda with their three daughters.

Breaking Barriers

Rick's efforts have helped tens of thousands of people and resulted in significant progress in treating spinal cord injuries. Moreover, Rick and his team have also helped break many barriers that have held back people with disabilities. Canadians have responded to Rick's efforts with new laws and programs that treat Canadians with disabilities with respect and equality. In return, many have been able to play leading roles in their country and communities.

In fact, in 1994, the Canadian Foundation for Physically Disabled Persons created the Terry Fox Hall of Fame in Toronto to recognize the efforts and achievements of "outstanding Canadians who have made extraordinary contributions to enriching the quality of life for people with physical disabilities."[2] Honorees have included Rick Hansen, Steven Fletcher, Chantal Petitclerc, Jeff Healey, Sam Sullivan, Cliff Chadderton (War Amps) and Whipper Billy Watson (Easter Seals). Several doctors have been noted as well. The Hall of Fame is another way for Canadians to celebrate and continue the work of people like Terry Fox and Rick Hansen for future generations.

Here are just a few brief thumbnail biographies of some of these outstanding Canadians.

Michael J. Fox

This Alberta-born, BC-raised Canadian is widely known as a lead actor in numerous movie and television roles, which include the wildly popular *Back to the Future* film trilogy, and the television series *Family Ties*

and *Spin City*. Later in life, Michael developed Parkinson's disease, but rather than retreating into the background, he became an advocate for sufferers. He also wrote several books describing his struggle with this cruelly debilitating disease and created a foundation to help generate funds and champion the cause.

Steven Fletcher

The Honourable Steven Fletcher was the first quadriplegic elected to the House of Commons in 2004, and was appointed to the Cabinet as Minister of State for Democratic Reform in 2008. A healthy outdoorsman, Steven's life was changed when the car he was in collided with a moose. He suffered a severe spinal cord injury that has left him paralyzed below the neck. However, he would not let his physical disability define his life, nor limit his options. He continues to lead an active outdoors life with the aid of numerous assistive devices and still plays an important role in the political life of Canada.

Jeff Healey

Although Jeff lost his sight to a rare form of cancer when he was just a baby, he moved far beyond this disability and enjoyed a stellar music career. He started playing guitar at the age of three and became a well-known rock and blues star, playing and recording with many famous musicians such as George Harrison of the Beatles. He also created his own jazz band, winning many admirers and awards. Jeff died from cancer in 2008. In 2009, he was inducted into the Terry Fox Hall of Fame.

Chantal Petitclerc

Chantal's life story is similar to Rick's. After losing the use of her legs when a barn door fell on her, she turned her attention and energy to sports. While at university, she trained in wheelchair sports and, like Rick, soon became a champion, winning two medals at the Barcelona Paralympic Games. During her brilliant career, she earned 21 Paralympic medals and won the Lou Marsh Trophy as Canada's athlete of the year in 2008. She also has a star on Canada's Walk of Fame in Toronto.

Barbara Turnbull

Barbara was a bright young eighteen-year-old girl working in a Toronto convenience store when she was shot in the course of a robbery. Although Barbara survived the attack, she suffered a severe spinal cord injury that left her paralyzed from the neck down. After graduating with a journalism degree, Barbara became a reporter for the *Toronto Star*. She also created the Barbara Turnbull Foundation, which funds research for spinal cord repair and regeneration.

Mayor Sam Sullivan

Sam Sullivan was an athletic young man from BC who broke his neck in a tragic ski accident when he was nineteen years old. At first Sam was severely depressed, even suicidal, when confronted with his disability. Facing life as a quadriplegic was almost too much. However, he turned his life around and became active both as an advocate for those suffering from disabilities and as a municipal politician. In 1993, he was elected to Vancouver City Council where he enjoyed a fifteen-year career. He was elected as mayor in 2005.

25th Anniversary Rick Hansen Relay

In 2010, Rick and his team realized it was time to celebrate the 25th anniversary of the Man In Motion World Tour. It was time to rekindle the fires that had launched their original journey, develop new programs, and revisit locations from the first tour. While the 25th Anniversary Relay would celebrate the achievements of Rick's generation, one of its aims was to inspire a new generation to continue the work.

Rick and his many associates aimed to achieve several milestones from 2010 to 2012, including a 25th anniversary relay across Canada. It was slated to begin on August 24, 2011, in Cape Spear, Newfoundland and Labrador and was to conclude in Vancouver, British Columbia, just as the first MIMWT had ended 25 years earlier.

Back in 1985, Rick had a young, untried team that was fueled by hope and conviction. In 2011, Rick was supported by major corporations, such as CTV, Air Canada, McDonald's and many others. The tour was managed by skilled organizers and supported by tens of thousands of well-wishers across the country.

Years after the accident, Rick and Don Alder are still great friends and avid fishermen. They are seen here at the 25th anniversary celebrations.

The plan was to cross Canada, but this time invite Canadians to participate and relive the dream of the Man In Motion World Tour.

The relay stretched 12,000 kilometres (7,456 miles) and touched 600 different communities. The campaign was led by Rick but carried out by 7,000 difference makers who retraced his steps.

Difference makers were chosen from thousands of applicants who were often inspirational figures in their own communities. These were people who made a difference. They walked, wheeled, biked, or somehow moved the special Rick Hansen Relay Medal from community to community, across Canada over a period of 9 months. They each received a replica of the commemorative medal.

The last stop in this successful relay was at the Terry Fox Plaza outside BC place on May 22, 2012. The campaign was completed that evening with a star-studded concert featuring musicians such as Jann Arden, Sarah McLaughlan, Marianas Trench and Johnny Reid. Presenters included Free The Children Founder, Craig Kielburger, and famed scientist and environmentalist, David Suzuki. The show was later broadcast nationally to an audience of millions. Patrick Roberge, the producer of the show noted that, "Rick's message now is: If one person can inspire many, imagine what we all can do together. So go out and make a difference."

Timeline

As for the future, Rick says, "What gives me hope and energy is the next generation. It's time for me to move from one Man In Motion to Many In Motion, to inspire new difference makers to dream big and make an impact. Extraordinary things can be accomplished by ordinary people every day. Together, we can make this moment the beginning of the greatest movement for positive change in our nation's history. If enough of us choose to change even one small thing, together we have the power to change anything. Together, anything is possible."

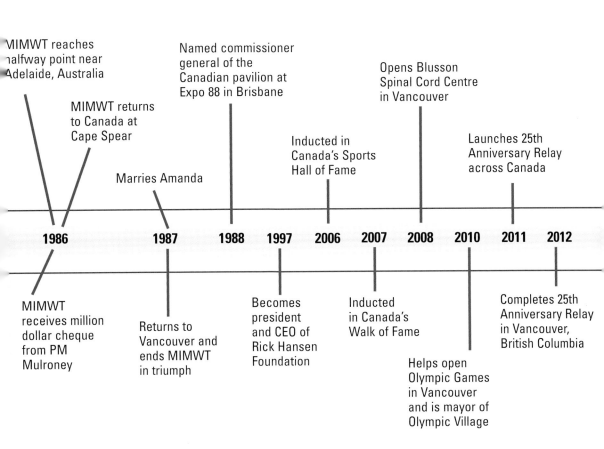

Awards

The Companion Order of Canada Order of British Columbia

Honorary Doctor of Laws degree from Carleton University, 2009

Fourteen honorary degrees bestowed

Her Majesty Queen Elizabeth II Golden Jubilee Commemorative
Medal, 2002

Athlete of the Century BC Wheelchair Sports, 2000

University of British Columbia Athletic Hall of Fame

WAC Bennett Award, BC Sports Hall of Fame

Lou Marsh/Canadian Outstanding Athlete of the Year Award; co-winner,
Wayne Gretzky

Outstanding Athlete of the Year, Canadian Wheelchair Sports Association

Manning Award for Innovations (National)

Outstanding Young Person of the World, Junior Chamber International

Achievements

Induction into the BC Sports Hall of Fame

Star on Canada's Walk of Fame

Recipient of CPA Alberta's Christopher Reeve Award

Induction into Canada's Sports Hall of Fame

Founded the Rick Hansen Institute

Established the Fraser River Sturgeon Conservation Society

National Partner in 2nd National Access Awareness Week

Initiated National Access Awareness Week

Set World Record for Longest Wheelchair Marathon (24,901.55 miles
or 40,000 kilometres), Guinness Book of Records

Appointments

Mayor of the Olympic Village, 2010 Olympic and Paralympic
Winter Games

Ambassador of the Edmonton 2005 World Masters Games

Secretary to Her Majesty Queen Elizabeth, 1989 visit to Canada

Commissioner General to Canada Pavilion at Expo '88 in Brisbane, Australia

(All information from Rick Hansen Foundation)

Endnotes

Chapter 1

1. Rick Hansen and Jim Taylor, *Rick Hansen: Man in Motion* (Vancouver: Douglas & MacIntyre Ltd. 1987), 9.

Chapter 2

1. Rick Hansen and Jim Taylor, *Rick Hansen: Man in Motion* (Vancouver: Douglas & MacIntyre Ltd. 1987), 8-9.

1. Rick Hansen and Jim Taylor, *Rick Hansen: Man in Motion* (Vancouver: Douglas & MacIntyre Ltd. 1987), 13.

Chapter 3

1. Rick Hansen and Jim Taylor, *Rick Hansen: Man in Motion* (Vancouver: Douglas & MacIntyre Ltd. 1987), 39.

2. Rick Hansen and Jim Taylor, *Rick Hansen: Man in Motion* (Vancouver: Douglas & MacIntyre Ltd. 1987), 33.

Chapter 4

1. Rick Hansen and Jim Taylor, *Rick Hansen: Man in Motion* (Vancouver: Douglas & MacIntyre Ltd. 1987), 48.

2. Rick Hansen and Dr. Joan Laub, *Going the Distance: Seven Steps To Personal Change* (Vancouver: Douglas & MacIntyre Ltd. 1994), 20.

Chapter 6

1. Rick Hansen and Jim Taylor, *Rick Hansen: Man in Motion* (Vancouver: Douglas & MacIntyre Ltd. 1987), 150.

Chapter 8

1. "The Zoomer list: Top 45 over 45," *Zoomer Magazine,* September 27, 2010, www.zoomermag.com.

Chapter 9

1. Rick Hansen and Dr. Joan Laub, *Going the Distance: Seven Steps To Personal Change* (Vancouver: Douglas & MacIntyre Ltd. 1994), iv.

2. Canadian Foundation for Physically Disabled Persons (CFPDP), "Canadian Disability Hall of Fame," 2011, http://cfpdp.com.

Bibliography

Hansen, Rick and Jim Taylor.
Rick Hansen: Man in Motion, Vancouver: Douglas & MacIntyre Ltd. 1987

Hansen, Rick and Dr. Joan Laub
Going the Distance: Seven Steps To Personal Change
Vancouver: Douglas & MacIntyre Ltd. 1994

Hansen scales the Great Wall of China
www.archives.cbc.ca/sports/exploits/clips/4116/

Rick Hansen completes his Man In Motion World Tour
www.archives.cbc.ca/sports/exploits/clips/779/

Rick Hansen: Man In Motion
www.archives.cbc.ca/sports/exploits/clips/698/

Rick Hansen discusses his autobiography
www.archives.cbc.ca/sports/exploits/clips/4118/

Man In Motion tour 2002—The Sequel
www.archives.cbc.ca/sports/exploits/clips/4107/

Rick Hansen Foundation
www.rickhansen.com

Image Credits

Index